WARRIORS

SKYCLAN & THE STRANGER

#1: THE RESCUE

WARRIORS
SKYCLAN & THE STRANGER
#1: THE RESCUE

CREATED BY
ERIN HUNTER

WRITTEN BY
DAN JOLLEY

ART BY
JAMES L. BARRY

HAMBURG // LONDON // LOS ANGELES // TOKYO

HARPER
An Imprint of HarperCollins Publishers

Warriors: SkyClan and the Stranger Vol. 1:
The Rescue
Created by Erin Hunter
Written by Dan Jolley
Art by James L. Barry

Lettering - John Hunt
Cover Design - Louis Csontos

Editor - Lillian Diaz-Przybyl
Managing Editor - Vy Nguyen
Print-Production Manager - Lucas Rivera
Art Director - Al-Insan Lashley
Director of Sales and Manufacturing - Allyson DeSimone
President and C.O.O. - John Parker
C.E.O. and Chief Creative Officer - Stu Levy

A  Manga

TOKYOPOP and 👁 are trademarks or registered trademarks of TOKYOPOP Inc.

TOKYOPOP Inc.
5900 Wilshire Blvd. Suite 2000
Los Angeles, CA 90036

E-mail: info@TOKYOPOP.com
Come visit us online at www.TOKYOPOP.com

For information address HarperCollins Children's Books, a division of HarperCollins Publishers,
10 East 53rd Street, New York, NY 10022.
www.harpercollinschildrens.com

ISBN 978-0-06-200836-7
Library of Congress catalog card number: 2011924605

11 12 13 14 15   LP/BV   10 9 8 7 6 5 4 3 2 1
❖
First Edition

Dear readers,

If you've read one of my mangas before, you'll know that as well as making the stories independent from the rest of the Warriors series, I also use them to fill in gaps, reveal more about characters who haven't taken center stage before, and even give away secrets from the past. This trilogy came about because I was reluctant to leave SkyClan at the end of their adventures in *SkyClan's Destiny*.

SkyClan is the mysterious fifth Clan of warrior cats, banished long, long ago from the forest when their territory was swallowed up by a Twoleg housing development. In *Firestar's Quest*, SkyClan's ancient leader, Cloudstar, visited Firestar in a dream and begged him to find the place where they had tried to make a home and rebuild the Clan. Firestar and Sandstorm traveled upriver from the forest to the deep sandy gorge where SkyClan had settled all those moons ago. The ThunderClan warriors found cats living nearby with hunting and fighting instincts that had lasted through generations, and gathered them to build a new SkyClan, with pride in their ancestors and a desire to live by the warrior code.

We returned to the gorge in *SkyClan's Destiny*, this time without Firestar and Sandstorm. The young Clan faced fresh challenges from curious dogs, stray Twolegs, and rivals prowling on the border. Under the leadership of Leafstar, SkyClan thrived, but winning one battle doesn't mean there isn't another one just around the corner. Leafstar may be deeply loyal to her Clan and to the warrior code, but she didn't grow up in a Clan, and neither did her Clanmates. Their inexperience makes them vulnerable; there are no elders to tell them what has been done before, no traditions that bind them to the gorge. When a crisis comes, Leafstar and her Clanmates will have to rely on what they have learned from Firestar and Sandstorm, as well as their faith that the new SkyClan can survive.

So what happened next? You're about to find out . . .

Best wishes always,
Erin Hunter

MY NAME IS LEAFSTAR.

I'M LEADER OF SKYCLAN.

SKYCLAN HASN'T EXISTED FOR THAT LONG. WE'RE STABLE NOW, BUT IT HASN'T BEEN EASY GETTING TO THIS POINT.

MY MATE, BILLYSTORM, IS WITH ME.

HE'S WHAT'S CALLED A DAYLIGHT-WARRIOR. HE'S A SKYCLAN WARRIOR DURING THE DAY...

...BUT AT NIGHT, HE GOES HOME TO HIS TWOLEGS AND STAYS WITH THEM IN THEIR NEST.

I WOULDN'T BE WHERE I AM TODAY WITHOUT HIS HELP.

7

WE'RE BEING CAREFUL!

WHOOPS...

OW!

WAK

ARE YOU ALL RIGHT? BIRDPAW! SAY SOMETHING!

UH... "SOMETHING"?

PFFF. WHAT DID I TELL YOU? DID I NOT JUST SAY TO WATCH YOURSELF UP THERE?

DID THOSE WORDS NOT JUST COME OUT OF MY MOUTH?

...YES...

RABBITLEAP! DON'T YOU REALIZE HOW YOUNG THEY ARE?

YOU PUSH THEM TOO MUCH, AND THIS HAPPENS!

SORRY...

11

I HEARD THAT SOMEONE BUMPED THEIR HEAD.

ECHOSONG IS OUR MEDICINE CAT. SHE'S VERY TALENTED. SKYCLAN IS LUCKY TO HAVE HER.

ALL RIGHT, NOW, LOOK AT ME...LET ME SEE HERE...

LOOKS LIKE A SIMPLE SCRAPE.

COME ALONG, BIRDPAW.

I'LL HAVE YOU FEELING BETTER BEFORE YOU KNOW IT.

BET I WON'T FALL OFF.

BET YOU WILL!

BET I GET UP THERE BEFORE YOU DO!

BET YOU DON'T!

WE MARKED HOW FAR INTO SKYCLAN TERRITORY THE SCENT CAME BY BENDING DOWN SMALL BRANCHES ON SOME OF THE TREES.

REALLY? I WOULDN'T HAVE THOUGHT OF THAT.

THAT'S A VERY GOOD TACTIC.

IT WAS EBONYCLAW'S IDEA.

NOT BAD, I SUPPOSE...

...FOR A DAYLIGHT-WARRIOR.

SNIFF!

"NOT BAD"?

I'LL TELL YOU THE TRUTH, EBONYCLAW...

ANY WARRIOR WOULD BE PROUD TO THINK OF SOMETHING LIKE THAT.

DAYLIGHT OR OTHERWISE.

IT WAS NOTHING, REALLY.

I SAW MY TWOLEG DO SOMETHING SIMILAR WITH STICKS WHEN PART OF THE BACKYARD FLOODED.

YOU'VE DONE AN AMAZING THING HERE, LEAFSTAR.

OH, I DON'T KNOW.

I DO KNOW. YOU'VE UNITED THE CLAN. IT'S STILL ONLY A FEW SEASONS OLD, AND YET WE'RE STRONG NOW.

SKYCLAN'S FUTURE LOOKS SECURE AT LAST.

15

READY?

AFTER YOU.

EVERYTHING WORKING...FLOWING TOGETHER... PURE CLAN WARRIORS AND DAYLIGHT-WARRIORS IN HARMONY, SIDE BY SIDE.

SOMETIMES I CAN SCARCELY BELIEVE IT.

ALL RIGHT, THERE YOU GO.

AND REMEMBER, DON'T GET THE DRESSING WET, OR IT'LL FALL OFF.

I UNDERSTAND.

THANKS, ECHOSONG.

TELL ME YOU HAVEN'T BEEN HUNTING!

AND YOU CAUGHT A BIRD-- BY CLIMBING A TREE, NO DOUBT! YOU HAVE TO START TAKING MORE CARE!

ECHOSONG, CALM DOWN!

I'M NOT SICK! I'M JUST EXPECTING KITS.

AND WHY DIDN'T YOU STOP HER?

STOP HER?

WHEN CAN ANY CAT STOP LEAFSTAR?

YOU KNOW, CLOVERTAIL...I WILL ADMIT THAT SOMETIMES I THINK HAVING KITS IS GOING TO BE EVEN HARDER THAN LEADING A CLAN.

WELL, IT PROBABLY WILL BE, IF I'M BEING HONEST. EVEN WITH BILLYSTORM TO HELP YOU.

"BUT BELIEVE ME WHEN I TELL YOU, THERE'S NOTHING BETTER."

SHARPCLAW!

A WORD?

ABOUT THAT FOX TRAIL THE PATROL MENTIONED.

ARE YOU GOING TO CHECK IT YOURSELF?

WAIT, THOSE TWO? REALLY?

I HAVE TO SAY, I'M SURPRISED. SHARPCLAW HAS ALWAYS BEEN SO DEDICATED TO HIS DUTIES...

...I DON'T THINK I'VE EVER THOUGHT ABOUT HIM TAKING A MATE.

SOME CATS COULD SAY THE SAME THING ABOUT YOU.

I WONDER IF MANY OF THE OTHER CLAN LEADERS HAVE KITS?

THEY MUST.

IT'S AS MUCH UP TO THEM TO KEEP THEIR CLANS GOING AS ANY CAT.

IT RAISES THOUGHTS, THOUGH. DOUBTS.

WHAT IF...?

WHAT IF I'M TORN BETWEEN CARING FOR MY KITS AND CARING FOR MY CLANMATES?

WILL THE CLAN BE VULNERABLE IF MY ATTENTION IS DIVIDED?

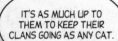

THE FOUR OF US TRACK THE YOUNG ONES. SOON WE REACH THE END OF THE FOX TRAIL, MARKED BY EBONYCLAW'S BRANCHES.

THE FOX'S TRAIL SEEMS TO DIVIDE, AS IF THE FOX HAS COME HERE ON TWO OCCASIONS FROM SEPARATE DIRECTIONS.

MISSING KITS ASIDE, I FIND THAT TROUBLING.

TINYCLOUD AND I WENT THIS WAY.

THEN LET'S FOLLOW THE OTHER TRAIL.

MY SENSES HAVE ALL SEEMED SUPERACUTE SINCE I FOUND OUT I WAS EXPECTING.

SO MUCH SO THAT I'M ABLE TO FOLLOW NETTLESPLASH AND SANDYPAW'S TRAIL THROUGH A PATCH OF WILD GARLIC.

THAT'S WHERE WASPWHISKER AND TINYCLOUD LOST THEM, NO DOUBT.

GETTING CLOSER...CLOSER...

THERE YOU ARE!

LEAFSTAR!

WHAT ARE YOU DOING OUT HERE?

LOOKING FOR YOU TWO. WHERE HAVE YOU BEEN?

OH, JUST—JUST IN THE WOODS, AH, TRYING TO FOLLOW THE FOX-SCENT.

YEAH, THE FOX-SCENT, BUT WE DIDN'T, UH, DIDN'T EVER FIND ANYTHING.

NOPE. NOTHING. NOTHING OUT HERE AT ALL.

IT WAS JUST SOME CROW-FOOD THAT WE FOUND--MAYBE THE FOX KILLED IT?

AND WE ONLY HAD A MOUTHFUL WHILE WE WERE LOOKING FOR SCENTS OF THE FOX...

I AM VERY DISAPPOINTED IN BOTH OF YOU. YOU KNOW BETTER.

WELL, BOTH OF YOU WILL BE PUNISHED, THERE'S NO QUESTION OF THAT.

I BELIEVE CHECKING LICHENFUR FOR TICKS AND CHANGING OUT HER BEDDING MOSS SHOULD BE SUITABLE.

EWWW!

I SUPPOSE SUCH FOOLISHNESS CAN BE FOUND IN ANY APPRENTICE.

THIS IS MUCH FARTHER THAN WE WERE SUPPOSED TO GO, LEAFSTAR.

LET'S HEAD BACK TO CAMP NOW. WHAT DO YOU SAY?

EACH SUNRISE, I FEEL BIGGER.

NEVER BEFORE HAVE I BEEN SO ENVIOUS OF CATS SENT ON PATROL.

IT'S A WONDER MY BELLY DOESN'T DRAG ON THE GROUND.

I BELIEVE I'LL PATROL A BIT MYSELF TODAY, SHARPCLAW. NOT A HUGE ONE, JUST SWING AROUND THE PERIMETER OF THE CAMP.

I'M AFRAID NOT, LEAFSTAR. I WON'T BE LETTING YOU PATROL AGAIN-- NOT UNTIL YOUR KITS ARE BORN.

WHAT?

I AM LEADER OF SKYCLAN! WHO ARE YOU TO TELL ME WHEN I CAN AND CAN'T DO SOMETHING?

WHO ARE YOU TO KEEP ME CAPTIVE?

WITH ALL DUE RESPECT, LEAFSTAR, DON'T BE RIDICULOUS. ANY OTHER QUEEN WOULD'VE BEEN CONFINED TO THE NURSERY BY NOW.

AND NO CAT IS KEEPING YOU PRISONER. YOU SIMPLY CAN'T PERFORM ALL YOUR USUAL WARRIOR DUTIES.

COME ON, LEAFSTAR. IT'S NOT AS THOUGH YOU CAN'T MOVE AT ALL.

IN FACT, I COULD USE SOME HELP GATHERING HERBS. WANT TO COME WITH ME?

ECHOSONG'S REQUEST IS A PAINFULLY TRANSPARENT EXCUSE TO MAKE ME FEEL USEFUL.

...ALL RIGHT.

BUT I KNOW SHE AND SHARPCLAW HAVE THE BEST OF INTENTIONS.

THAT'S WHAT I KEEP TELLING MYSELF, IN ANY CASE.

LEAFSTAR!

I'M SO SORRY I'M LATE GETTING TO THE GORGE!

MY HOUSEFOLK ACCIDENTALLY SHUT ME IN. I HAD TO WRIGGLE OUT OF A TINY WINDOW.

HA-HA-HA... I THOUGHT YOU LOOKED A BIT SQUEEZED.

BUT, BUT ARE YOU— WERE YOU UP HERE LOOKING FOR ME?

IS SOMETHING WRONG?

IF SOMETHING WERE WRONG WITH LEAFSTAR, SHE'D HARDLY STAGGER ALL THE WAY TO TWOLEGPLACE TO TELL YOU ABOUT IT.

BUT, WELL, YOU WOULD SEND SOMEONE, WOULDN'T YOU?

I PROMISE, IF THERE'S ANY TROUBLE, WE WILL.

EVEN IF IT'S THE MIDDLE OF THE NIGHT.

MAYBE I'M NOT THE ONLY CAT TORN IN TWO WAYS BY THESE KITS.

COME ON, LET'S GO BACK TO CAMP.

THE HERB SELECTION UP HERE IS PITIFUL.

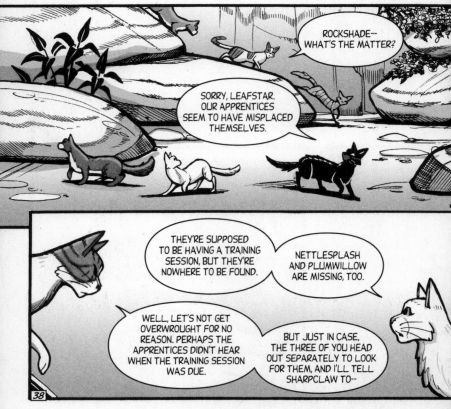

ROCKSHADE-- WHAT'S THE MATTER?

SORRY, LEAFSTAR. OUR APPRENTICES SEEM TO HAVE MISPLACED THEMSELVES.

THEY'RE SUPPOSED TO BE HAVING A TRAINING SESSION, BUT THEY'RE NOWHERE TO BE FOUND.

NETTLESPLASH AND PLUMWILLOW ARE MISSING, TOO.

WELL, LET'S NOT GET OVERWROUGHT FOR NO REASON. PERHAPS THE APPRENTICES DIDN'T HEAR WHEN THE TRAINING SESSION WAS DUE.

BUT JUST IN CASE, THE THREE OF YOU HEAD OUT SEPARATELY TO LOOK FOR THEM, AND I'LL TELL SHARPCLAW TO--

WHICH IS WHAT LEADS ME HERE.

THE SUN THE NEXT DAY IS EVEN HOTTER THAN THE DAY BEFORE. SIMPLY LYING IN THE SHADE ISN'T ENOUGH.

WHERE I SOON FIND MORE THAN JUST RELIEF FROM THE HEAT.

I DON'T SEE WHY I CAN'T TELL TINYCLOUD-- IT COULD HELP THE CLAN!

NO, YOU CAN'T!

YOU MUSTN'T!

THIS IS OUR SECRET. IF WE TELL ANYONE ELSE, IT'LL SPOIL EVERYTHING.

CLOVERTAIL ALWAYS SAID SECRETS SHOULD BE TOLD IF THEY MADE ANYONE FEEL BAD.

AND THIS SECRET IS STARTING TO MAKE ME FEEL BAD!

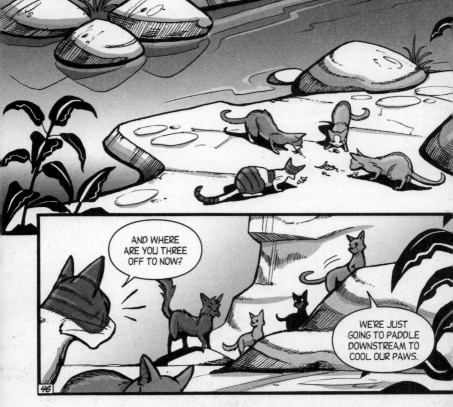

WELL, AT LEAST NETTLESPLASH HAS GOTTEN OVER HIS FEAR OF WATER.

HE'S NEVER LIKED IT, NOT SINCE PLUMWILLOW PUSHED HIM IN WHEN THEY WERE KITS.

I BELIEVE I'LL GO DIP MY PAWS AS WELL.

NOW WE'LL SEE WHAT'S WHAT.

CAREFUL IN THE WATER, LEAFSTAR!

YES--YOU DON'T WANT TO SINK UNDER THE WEIGHT OF THAT BELLY!

I WAS HOPING IT WOULD HELP ME FLOAT!

HA-HA-HA!

...BUT THEN IT FEELS AS IF ALL THE AIR IS KNOCKED OUT OF ME.

HELLO, MY PRETTIES! HOW ARE YOU TODAY?

I SEE YOUR EYE IS MUCH BETTER, FLOSSIE.

THAT ANTIBIOTIC OINTMENT REALLY DID THE TRICK, DIDN'T IT?

SO NICE OF THE VETERINARIAN TO LET ME HAVE SOME.

BE BACK IN A MOMENT, DEARIES!

NETTLESPLASH! BIRDPAW! ALL OF YOU!

I CAN'T BELIEVE WHAT I'M SEEING!

YOU ARE ALL CLANBORN CATS, NOT KITTYPETS! NOT EVEN DAYLIGHT-WARRIORS! AND THE WOODS ARE FULL OF PREY.

NEWLEAF HAS BEEN KIND TO US. WHY DO YOU WANT TO BE FED BY A TWOLEG AS IF YOU CAN'T HUNT FOR YOURSELVES?

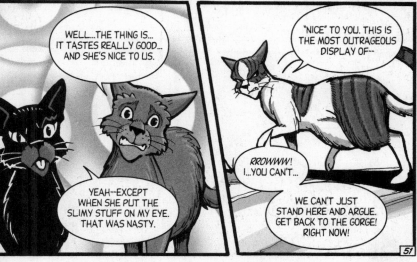

WELL...THE THING IS... IT TASTES REALLY GOOD... AND SHE'S NICE TO US.

YEAH--EXCEPT WHEN SHE PUT THE SLIMY STUFF ON MY EYE. THAT WAS NASTY.

"NICE" TO YOU. THIS IS THE MOST OUTRAGEOUS DISPLAY OF--

RROWWW! I...YOU CAN'T...

WE CAN'T JUST STAND HERE AND ARGUE. GET BACK TO THE GORGE! RIGHT NOW!

THE PAIN...IN MY STOMACH...
IT'S LIKE NOTHING I'VE EVER
FELT BEFORE...

WHAT'S HAPPENING TO ME?

LEAFSTAR! ARE
YOU ALL RIGHT?

NO, I'M NOT ALL
RIGHT! ARE YOU
BLIND?!

SOMETHING'S
WRONG!

53

55

MAKE SURE YOU'RE OUT OF ANY DANGER!

BILLYSTORM! TELL NETTLESPLASH!

HE'LL KNOW WHERE I AM!

SHAMEFUL, A MAMA CAT HAVING HER KITS IN A GORGE LIKE THAT.

WHAT IS THIS PLACE?

DON'T BELIEVE SHE MEANS TO HURT US, SO I KEEP MY CLAWS SHEATHED.

I CAN SEE THE WAY OUT FROM HERE.

IT'S WORSE THAN NOT HAVING A WAY OUT AT ALL.

SKRITCH SKRITCH

SKRITCH SKRITCH

HUH?

OH LOOK, HARRY'S COME HOME!

HAVE YOU BEEN HUNTING, MY BRAVE BOY?

CLICK

EVERYONE, THIS IS HARRY.

HARRY, THESE ARE OUR NEW VISITORS. THEY HAVEN'T TOLD ME WHAT THEIR NAMES ARE YET.

YOU'RE ONE OF THOSE WILD CATS THAT LIVE IN THE GORGE, RIGHT?

IT'S SKYCLAN. THAT'S THE NAME OF OUR GROUP. AND I'M THEIR LEADER, LEAFSTAR.

YOU DON'T LOOK LIKE MUCH OF A LEADER RIGHT NOW. ARE THOSE YOUR KITS?

OF COURSE THEY ARE!

WHY DID YOU BRING THEM HERE?

I DIDN'T. I WAS STOLEN BY YOUR TWOLEG, ALONG WITH MY NEW LITTER!

WHY DIDN'T YOU RUN AWAY? SHE CAN'T RUN VERY FAST, YOU KNOW.

I COULDN'T ABANDON MY KITS!

HELP US, BILLYSTORM. CAN YOU HEAR ME? WHY HAVEN'T YOU COME FOR US?

I'M SENDING MY THOUGHTS TO YOU. HELP US.

PLEASE.

ALL RIGHT, LITTLE ONES, HERE'S YOUR BREAKFAST...

AND I'VE GOT SOME NICE CLEAN THINGS FOR YOU TO SLEEP ON...

OH, AREN'T THEY JUST PERFECT?

YOU'RE A LUCKY GIRL, AREN'T YOU, LITTLE MISS MAMA CAT?

THIS IS WRONG...I WAS SUPPOSED TO NAME THEM, WITH BILLYSTORM, BY NOW.

SHOULD I NAME THEM MYSELF?

BUT WHAT IF WE'RE STUCK HERE FOREVER?

GOOD MORNING, LEAFSTAR.

GOOD FOR YOU, MAYBE.

WE'RE PRISONERS HERE.

ALL THIS ENERGY YOU SPEND, WANTING TO GET BACK TO YOUR CLAN.

WHAT'S SO GREAT ABOUT IT?

HARRY SEEMS A TINY BIT FRIENDLIER THIS MORNING...

...SO, TO TAKE MY MIND OFF THINGS, I START TO TELL HIM MORE ABOUT LIFE IN SKYCLAN.

BUT I'VE NEVER BEEN HAPPIER TO BE INTERRUPTED!

SHARPCLAW!

LEAFSTAR!

ARE YOU ALL RIGHT? ARE THE KITS ALL RIGHT?

I'M FINE, THE KITS ARE FINE, BUT...

...WE NEED TO GET OUT!

WE'RE COMING UP WITH A PLAN!

DON'T WORRY, WE'LL GET YOU OUT OF THERE!

SO YOUR CLANMATES CAME ALL THIS WAY TO RESCUE YOU?

OF COURSE THEY DID! I'M THEIR LEADER!

HMM. I'M IMPRESSED.

OH MY!

HAVE YOU COME TO SEE YOUR FRIEND?

SHE'S FINE NOW, AND ALL THE KITS ARE DOING JUST WONDERFULLY.

HERE, LET ME GET SOMETHING FOR YOU!

HOW ABOUT A NICE BOWL OF MILK? WOULD YOU LIKE THAT?

WARRIORS!

COME ON-- WE HAVE TO GO!

THEY'RE HERE...MY CLAN KNOWS EXACTLY WHERE I AM NOW...AND YET I FEEL MORE ALONE THAN EVER.

• • •

OH, COME NOW, LEAFSTAR. IT'S NOT ALL BAD.

LOOK, THE TWOLEG GAVE US TUNA TONIGHT. HAVE YOU EVER HAD TUNA BEFORE?

I CAN'T EVEN BRING MYSELF TO SPEAK TO HARRY, EVEN THOUGH HE'S TRYING TO HELP, IN HIS OWN WAY.

WHAT ARE WE GOING TO DO?

TWO LONG DAYS PASS, WITH NO SIGN OF MY CLANMATES.

THEY WOULDN'T ABANDON US... WOULD THEY?

MY APPETITE IS GONE COMPLETELY. I EAT ONLY WHEN I FORCE MYSELF TO.

EVEN THE "TUNA" HARRY GOT SO EXCITED ABOUT TASTES LIKE ASH IN MY MOUTH.

I'M SORRY, LEAFSTAR, I JUST DON'T UNDERSTAND.

IT'S NICE HERE. IT'S WARM, AND COMFORTABLE, AND SAFE.

WHY DO YOU WANT TO GO BACK TO SKYCLAN SO BADLY?

THIS TIME I FINALLY DESCRIBE EVERYTHING FOR HARRY.

EVERYTHING I LOVE ABOUT LIFE IN SKYCLAN.

THE FRIENDSHIP, THE SELF-SUFFICIENCY, THE LOYALTY, THE FREEDOM.

THE RUSH OF CATCHING YOUR OWN PREY...

...THE GLOW THAT COMES FROM KNOWING AN ENTIRE CLAN WOULD DIE FOR YOU.

AND YET...I AM STILL TRAPPED HERE, IN THIS TWOLEG NEST. WORSE YET...

...MY KITS' EYES HAVE BEGUN TO OPEN. I DON'T WANT THE FIRST THING THEY SEE TO BE A TWOLEG NEST!

WHAT IF THEY THINK THEY'RE KITTYPETS?

I TRY TO SHOW THEM. SHOW THEM THE OUTDOORS, THE GRASS, THE SKY...BUT IT DOESN'T WORK AT ALL.

OWW! MAMA, THAT PINCHES MY FUR!

PUT ME DOWN, PUT ME DOWN!

IT FEELS AS IF EVERY-THING IS SLIDING AWAY FROM ME HERE...

OH DEAR! WHAT HAVE YOU DONE TO YOUR POOR LEG?

YOU POOR THING! I'LL HAVE YOU FIXED UP IN NO TIME.

YOU CAN STAY THE NIGHT, BUT I'M AFRAID I CAN'T LET YOU GO INTO THE SITTING ROOM.

WE ALREADY HAVE SOME GUESTS IN THERE. NOW HERE YOU GO SOME NICE FOOD AND SOME MILK.

IN THE MORNING WE'LL TAKE A LOOK AT THAT LEG, AND SEE IF YOU NEED TO GO TO MR. VETERINARIAN, WON'T WE?

CLICK

LEAFSTAR! I'M OKAY! I WAS JUST PRETENDING TO HAVE A BAD LEG SO THE TWOLEG WOULD LET ME IN!

THE OTHERS ARE OUTSIDE. I'M GOING TO GET YOU OUT OF HERE!

MY DEN HAS NEVER, EVER BEEN AS COMFORTABLE AS IT WAS LAST NIGHT.

ESPECIALLY SINCE BILLYSTORM STAYED THE WHOLE NIGHT WITH US. HE CAN'T DO THAT VERY OFTEN.

AND NOW IT'S TIME TO SEE IF I CAN BRING THE CLAN BACK TO NORMAL.

CLOVERTAIL WATCHES OVER MY KITS FOR ME WHILE I SPEAK.

"WHAT'S SO GREAT ABOUT YOUR CLAN?" HARRY ASKED.

THAT'S WHAT'S SO GREAT ABOUT MY CLAN. WE WORK TOGETHER. WE ARE ONE.

I'M PROUD TO BE THE LEADER OF A STRONG CLAN THAT LOOKS OUT FOR ALL ITS CATS, YOUNG AND OLD, BIG AND SMALL.

...I WON'T EVER LET MYSELF BE CAUGHT OFF GUARD BY A TWOLEG AGAIN.

I ALSO NEED TO THANK FALLOWFERN FOR HER BRILLIANT PLAN...

OH--ACTUALLY THAT WAS BIRDPAW'S IDEA.

SHE THOUGHT THE TWOLEG PUT THAT GREASY STUFF ON HER EYE TO HELP IT...

WELL, BIRDPAW, IT WAS AN EXCELLENT IDEA...

...BUT YOU MUST ALSO REMEMBER, ALWAYS, THAT YOU ARE A CLAN CAT...YOU AND THE REST OF THE APPRENTICES...

...AND THAT YOU NEVER TAKE FOOD FROM TWOLEGS.

BY THE WAY... I'VE THOUGHT OF SOME NAMES.

OH? WHAT HAVE YOU COME UP WITH?

I HOPE YOU LIKE THEM...

FIREKIT FOR OUR LITTLE GINGER SHE-CAT... AND STORMKIT FOR THE GRAY-AND-GINGER SHE-CAT. AFTER FIRESTAR AND SANDSTORM.

AND FOR THE GRAY TOM... HARRYKIT, AFTER THE CAT WHO HELPED US ESCAPE FROM THE TWOLEG.

I DO LIKE THOSE.

HELLO?

HARRY!

I DECIDED TO COME AND SEE WHAT ALL THE FUSS WAS ABOUT.

IF LIFE IN SKYCLAN IS SO GOOD, PERHAPS I SHOULD JOIN YOU.

YOU REALIZE, YOU'D HAVE TO TRAIN TO BE A WARRIOR. JUST AS WE ALL DID.

OF COURSE.

WELL, YOU'D... YOU'D BE WELCOME, OF COURSE...

YOU'LL LEARN TO HUNT FOR US, GUARD THE BORDERS, BE WILLING TO GIVE UP YOUR LIFE FOR YOUR CLANMATES.

I'M WILLING TO LEARN WHAT I NEED TO.

WELL, THEN... WELCOME TO SKYCLAN!

ACTUALLY, THERE'S SOMEONE YOU NEED TO MEET, FOR THE SECOND TIME.

THIS IS HARRYKIT.

I HOPE YOU DON'T MIND, WE NAMED HIM AFTER YOU.

HARRY'S NOT MY REAL NAME.

THAT'S JUST WHAT THE TWOLEG CALLS ME.

TO BE CONTINU

ERIN HUNTER

is inspired by a love of cats and a fascination with the ferocity of the natural world. As well as having great respect for nature in all its forms, Erin enjoys creating rich, mythical explanations for animal behavior. She is also the author of the Seekers series.

Download the free Warriors app and chat on Warriors message boards at www.warriorcats.com.

For exclusive information on your favorite authors and artists, visit www.authortracker.com.

The #1 national bestselling series, now in manga!

WARRIORS

SKYCLAN & THE STRANGER

BEYOND THE CODE

TOKYOPOP

HARPER COLLINS

ERIN HUNTER

2

SKYCLAN'S ADVENTURES
CONTINUE IN

WARRIORS

SKYCLAN & THE STRANGER
#2: BEYOND THE CODE

Leafstar was able to escape from the Twoleg's home
with the help of Billystorm and her Clanmates, but
more trouble lies ahead. Sol has joined SkyClan's ranks
and, unbeknownst to Leafstar, is subtly working to
sabotage the warrior code. When Sol's actions lead to a
disaster for the Clan, Leafstar must determine whether
or not to trust the stranger in her ranks—at the risk of
jeopardizing SkyClan's future.

WARRIORS

THE LOST WARRIOR

WARRIOR'S REFUGE

WARRIOR'S RETURN

Find out what really happened to Graystripe when he was captured by Twolegs, and follow him and Millie on their torturous journey through the old forest territory and Twolegplace to find ThunderClan.

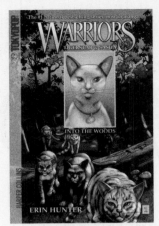

The #1 national bestselling series, now in manga!

WARRIORS

TIGERSTAR & SASHA

INTO THE WOODS

HARPER COLLINS

ERIN HUNTER

The #1 national bestselling series, now in manga!

WARRIORS

TIGERSTAR & SASHA

ESCAPE FROM
THE FOREST

HARPER COLLINS

ERIN HUNTER

The #1 national bestselling series, now in manga!

WARRIORS

TIGERSTAR & SASHA

RETURN TO THE CLANS

HARPER COLLINS

ERIN HUNTER

SASHA'S STORY
IS REVEALED IN

WARRIORS

TIGERSTAR AND SASHA

Sasha has everything she wants: kind housefolk who take care of her during the day, and the freedom to explore the woods beyond Twolegplace at night. But when Sasha is forced to leave her home, she must forge a solitary new life in the forest. When Sasha meets Tigerstar, leader of ShadowClan, she begins to think that she may be better off joining the ranks of his forest Clan. But Tigerstar has many secrets, and Sasha must decide whether she can trust him.

RAVENPAW FIGHTS TO
DEFEND HIS HOME IN

WARRIORS

RAVENPAW'S PATH

#1: SHATTERED PEACE

#2: A CLAN IN NEED

#3: THE HEART OF A WARRIOR

Ravenpaw has settled into life on the farm, away from the forest and Tigerstar's evil eye. He knows that leaving the warrior Clans was the right choice, and he appreciates his quiet days and peaceful nights with his best friend, Barley. But when five rogue cats from Twolegplace come to the barn seeking shelter, Ravenpaw and Barley are forced to flee their new home. With the help of ThunderClan, Ravenpaw and Barley must try to find a way to overpower the rogues—before they lose their home for good.

The #1 national bestselling series, now in manga!

WARRIORS

THE RISE OF SCOURGE

TOKYOPOP®

HARPER COLLINS

ERIN HUNTER

WARRIORS

THE RISE OF
SCOURGE

Black-and-white Tiny may be the runt of the litter, but
he's also the most curious about what lies beyond the
backyard fence. When he crosses paths with some wild
cats defending their territory, Tiny is left with scars—
and a bitter, deep-seated grudge—that he carries with
him back to Twolegplace. As his reputation grows
among the strays and loners that live in the dirty brick
alleyways, Tiny leaves behind his name, his kittypet
past, and everything that was once important to him—
except his deadly desire for revenge.

WARRIORS

SUPER EDITION

CROOKEDSTAR'S PROMISE

EXCLUSIVE MANGA ADVENTURE INSIDE!

ERIN HUNTER

TURN THE PAGE FOR A SNEAK PEEK AT

WARRIORS

SUPER EDITION

CROOKEDSTAR'S PROMISE

Crookedkit dreams of becoming a great Clan leader. Then a mysterious cat appears in his dreams, whispering promises of greatness and glory—if only he will pledge his undying loyalty to RiverClan. But what seems like a harmless promise could prove to be his downfall. . . .

CHAPTER 1

Stormkit edged farther along the slippery branch. Volekit's dare rang in his ears. *Bet you fall off before you get to the end!*

He unsheathed his claws and dug them into the frozen bark. From here, he could see a long way downstream, as far as the bend in the river. He could just glimpse the first of the stepping-stones beyond. And on the far shore, Sunningrocks! Its sheer side shadowed the water and its wide, smooth stone summit sparkled with frost. Stormkit fluffed out his fur. He'd seen farther than any other kit in the Clan! They'd never even seen past the reed bed.

"Be careful!" Oakkit called from the camp clearing.

"Shut up, Oakkit! I'm a warrior!" Stormkit looked down, past the fat, mouse-brown bulrush heads, into the dense forest of reeds that jutted out of the icy river. Minnows flitted between the stems, their scales flashing.

Could he reach down with a paw, break the thin ice, and scoop them out? He pressed his pale brown belly to the bark, wrapped his hind legs around the narrow branch, and swung his forepaws down toward the tiny fish. Tingling with frustration, he felt his claws brush the tips of the bulrushes. *I was born in a storm! I'm going to be Clan leader one day!* Stormkit stretched harder, trembling with the effort.

"What are you doing?" Oakkit yelped.

"Let him be!" Stormkit heard Rainflower silencing Oakkit, a purr rumbling in her throat. "Your brother has the courage of a warrior already."

Stormkit clung tighter to the branch. *I'll be fine. I'm stronger than StarClan.*

"Look out!" Oakkit squeaked.

A rush of wind tugged Stormkit's fur. A flurry of black-and-white feathers battered his ears.

Magpie!

Talons scraped his spine.

Frog dirt and fish guts! Stormkit's claws were wrenched out of the bark. He plummeted into the reeds and crashed through the thin ice. The freezing water shocked the breath from him. Minnows darted away as he thrashed in the water.

Where's the shore? River water flooded his mouth. It tasted of stone and weeds. Spluttering, he struggled to swim, but the stiff reeds blocked his flailing paws. *StarClan, help me!* Panic shot through him as he fought to keep his muzzle above water.

Suddenly the stems beside him swished apart and Tanglewhisker plunged through.

"I'm okay!" Stormkit spluttered. Water rushed into his mouth again and he sank, coughing, beneath the ice.

Teeth gripped his scruff.

"Kits!"

Stormkit heard Tanglewhisker's muffled growl as the elder hauled him up.

Shivering with cold, Stormkit bunched his paws against

his belly, wincing with embarrassment as he swung from Tanglewhisker's jaws. Tanglewhisker pushed his way through the reeds and deposited Stormkit on the bank next to his mother.

"Nice dive, Stormkit!" Volekit teased.

"Like a kingfisher," Beetlekit added. "Maybe Hailstar should change your name to Birdbrain."

Stormkit growled at the two kits as they crowded around him. One moon older, they loomed over him like crows.

Echomist paced anxiously behind them, her soft gray fur fluffed with worry. "Don't tease, you two."

Petalkit pushed past her brothers. "*I* wasn't teasing!" The pretty tortoiseshell she-cat stuck her nose in the air. "I think he was brave to try!"

Purring, Rainflower licked Stormkit's ears. "Next time, grip the branch harder."

Stormkit shook her off. "Don't worry. I will."

As Tanglewhisker shook water from his long tabby pelt, Birdsong hurried down the slope from the elders' den. "You'll catch cold!" she scolded.

Tanglewhisker blinked at his tabby-and-white mate. "Did you want me to let him drown?"

"One of the warriors would have rescued him," Birdsong retorted.

Tanglewhisker shrugged. "They're busy."

Rainflower purred. "I think Stormkit would have found his own way out. He's a strong little cat, aren't you?"

Stormkit felt his fur glow with the warmth of his mother's praise. He blinked water out of his eyes and looked around the clearing. This was the home of RiverClan, the greatest Clan of all. He hadn't seen it before the flood, so the smooth brown mud that covered the ground and the heaps of battered wet reeds that cluttered every corner were more familiar to him than the densely woven walls and open spaces that were emerging. Timberfur and Cedarpelt were carrying bundles of freshly picked dry reeds across the clearing to Softpaw and Whitepaw, who were weaving them into the tattered apprentices' den. Farther along the river's edge, Shellheart and Ottersplash were gathering more stems. Fallowtail was helping Brambleberry clear the last of the muddy debris from the medicine den. Owlfur and Lakeshine were dragging deadwood and bark that had been washed through the reeds and into the clearing.

It had been a whole moon since the stormy night when Stormkit and Oakkit had been born, but the camp still showed signs of being swept away. Fortunately the elders' den had held firm and only needed a little re-weaving here and there. And the nursery, a ball of tightly overlapping willow branches and reeds, had been found downstream, wedged between the stepping-stones. It had been easy enough to drag it back to camp and lodge it among the thick sedge bushes. A few patches had repaired it, though it was still damp inside from the soaking. Rainflower tucked fresh moss into their nest every evening, but Stormkit still woke each morning with a cold, wet pelt.

Delve Deeper into the Clans

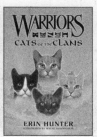

Warrior Cats Come to Life in Manga!